Fearsome Four

The Zombies of the Moonlit Marshes

Joseph Jethro

First published in Great Britain in 2024

ISBN: 978-1-917452-09-0

josephjethro45@outlook.com

Contents

Also By Joseph Jethro:

- Undercover Gangster: Blood Ties In The Shadows
- Secret Gangster: My Life Is All About Violence
- Triple Caste Gangster: He Never Told Her
- Never Underestimate Girls: Will She Ever Unlock The Truth or…
- Emric Ladislas: I Tried

Joseph Jethro's Children's Books:

- The Adventure of Numberland
- Oreo and Kiki: Kitchen Disaster
- Oreo and Kiki: Living Room Disaster
- Princess Lilly and the Forest Animals
- Princess Naila and the Sea Animals

Chapter One

The thick fog hung in the air, blanketing everything in a shroud of grey. Even if you stretched out your hand, it would vanish into the swirling grey. Overhead, the full moon loomed, its pale light struggling to pierce the misty haze, casting long, ghostly shadows. The wind roared furiously through the trees, shaking their branches and sending leaves swirling into the air.

Abner glanced over his shoulder, his eyes darting nervously through the fog. 'Come on, guys, hurry up!' he whispered, his voice barely rising above the ghostly whispers of the wind. He stood at the edge of the cracked road, where the fog was so thick it felt like it was closing in around him.

A car moved cautiously along the road, its headlights cutting through the murk like sharp knives. The beams made the fog twist and swirl, casting shadows that seemed to move on their own like ghosts creeping through the night. Abner quickly pulled his hoodie up, tugging it low over his face. He stayed motionless, holding his breath as the car drove past, its engine growling like a beast. Then, just as suddenly as it appeared, it vanished into the mist.

Soon, Ray and Sani caught up to Abner, their breath turning to mist in the chilly air.

'How do you know we're going the right way?' Sani asked, rubbing his frozen fingertips together and breathing on them to keep warm.

'Cause I've got a map, silly,' Abner said with a grin, pulling out a rolled-up map from his backpack. 'Here, shine the flashlight on it, will ya?' He gestured at Sani, holding the map open.

Sani switched on the flashlight, the beam bouncing across the foggy air before settling on the map.

'Whoa, that's so cool! Can I have it?' Ray asked, his eyes lighting up as he admired the intricate details sketched across the paper.

'Not a chance,' Abner replied, shaking his head at Ray, who had a habit of trying to snag his stuff.

Abner traced his finger to a section of the map. 'Okay, first, we've got to cross this road,' he said, glancing at the cracked pavement. 'Then we head through...this swamp,' he added, his tone dropping as he let out a long sigh, his breath turning into mist in the frosty air.

'A swamp? Yikes!' Ray exclaimed, raising an eyebrow. 'I hope there aren't any crocs...or swamp monsters,' he added, folding his arms and glaring at Abner.

'Take a chill pill,' Sani said with a shrug. 'There's no such thing as monsters.'

'Then why is Abner dragging us on this so-called hunt for zombies?' Ray asked, his voice dripping with disappointment.

'Because *he* believes they're real,' Sani replied, gesturing at Abner. 'And apparently, we're all just following him to find this 'marsh zombie' thing...'

Straightening up, Abner cut him off. '*The Zombies of the Moonlit Marshes*. That's what it's called,' he said with a proud smirk.

'Right, the Moonlit Marshes. Blah, blah, blah,' Sani retorted, rolling his eyes dramatically. 'We're gonna go there, take one look around, and prove to him there's no such thing as zombies,' he added, puffing out his cheeks in exaggerated annoyance.

'Ohhh,' Ray murmured, stretching the sound while nodding deliberately, his face a mix of scepticism and intrigue. 'Zombies aren't real? Yeah, I'm not convinced.'

'Where's Umari?' Abner asked, his eyes darting around the misty darkness.

'S-sorry!' a voice suddenly stammered, breaking the silence.

A moment later, a figure came crashing out of the bushes, landing flat on the ground with a loud *thud*.

Abner rolled his eyes and let out an impatient sigh. 'Come on, Umari, we don't have all night,' he said, grabbing him by the arm and hauling him to his feet.

They crossed the cracked road, the fog growing thicker with each step as if the world was slowly swallowing them whole. Abner led the way, his eyes scanning the path ahead, while Sani held the flashlight, the beam cutting through the mist but barely reaching beyond a few feet.

When they reached the edge of the swamp, the air turned colder. It was thick with a damp, musty scent that clung to their senses, like old leaves and wet earth. 'Okay, we've gotta roll up our pants,' Abner said, glancing at Ray and Sani. 'It's gonna get muddy, and we don't want to ruin them.'

Ray groaned. 'Great, swamp water and mud. Perfect.'

Sani sighed deeply but started tugging up his pants. 'Don't complain. We'll prove there are no zombies; then we can head back home.'

Umari hesitated, looking at the murky water. 'This feels...wrong,' he muttered, his voice almost lost in the howl of the wind.

Abner shot him a look, his eyebrow lifting in amusement. 'Scared, Umari? Come on, it's just a swamp.'

'I'm not scared,' Umari grumbled, though his voice didn't sound all that convincing. He rolled his pants up and stepped gingerly into the swamp, feeling the cold, sluggish water creep around his ankles.

The muck stubbornly clung to their feet while the air hummed with the chorus of croaking frogs and the persistent buzz of insects. Strange shapes loomed in the distance, half-hidden in the fog, but when they looked closely, they saw only twisted trees and tangled vines.

'I swear, this place is like a horror movie,' Ray muttered, his voice shaky. 'I'm pretty sure I saw something move over there...'

'Stop being a baby,' Sani snapped, though his voice wavered slightly. 'It's just the wind or something.' But even he couldn't hide the nervousness in his eyes.

Finally, they crossed the swamp and stepped into a deserted farmyard. The wind rustled the trees, making them jump, all of them half-expecting something to leap from the shadows. The farm was eerily quiet, with broken fences and old crates scattered around.

After what felt like forever, they reached the edge of the yard. The old, creaky wooden fence around the property looked like it had been standing there for years, barely held together by rusted nails. The barn in the distance was falling apart, its doors hanging crooked on their hinges.

'Let's get over this fence fast,' Abner whispered, glancing over at the creepy barn.

They moved quickly, stepping over broken planks and old tools on the ground. They jumped over the creaky fence, their eyes scanning the dark shadows and their hearts pounding with every step.

Finally, they reached the marsh. The ground was soft and spongy, covered in tangled roots and tall, swaying reeds. A damp, unpleasant smell hung in the air, and the thick mist made it impossible to see far ahead.

Abner looked at the map again. 'This is it,' he whispered, stepping forward. 'The Moonlit Marshes.'

Chapter Two

'Hey, guys,' Abner muttered, pulling his coat tighter around himself. 'I'm freezing my twinkle toes off.'

Ray snorted from the back of the group. 'Well, I'm freezing my butt off. Pretty sure it's gonna fall off and roll into the mud.'

Sani groaned. 'Do you *ever* stop talking about your butt?'

'I'm serious!' Ray shot back. 'If it falls off, one of you will be carrying it!'

Umari shivered, glancing around like a nervous owl. 'Uh, guys, do you really think this is a good idea?' His voice quivered as he hugged himself.

'This is the *best* idea,' Abner whispered, his eyes gleaming. 'Don't you want to be the first kid to see the zombies of the Moonlit Marshes?'

'I don't think zombies are real,' Sani said, gripping the flashlight so tightly his knuckles turned white.

'Y-yeah,' Umari mumbled, his teeth clattering. 'Z-zombies aren't real. R-right?'

'Oh, they're real,' Abner hissed, his voice dropping into a spooky tone. He lifted his hands and made a grotesque face. 'They creep up on you when you least expect it...and then BOOM!' He clapped his hands together loudly, making everyone jump.

'STOP THAT!' Umari shrieked, diving behind Sani. 'That's not funny!'

'Oh, but it *is* funny,' Abner said, grinning. 'They'll grab you when you're not looking and gobble you up like a late-night snack!'

'Th-that sounds...t-t-terrible!' Umari stammered, peeking out from behind Sani.

'C'mon, Abner,' Sani said with a stern look. 'Stop scaring your little brother.'

Ray snickered, doubling over with laughter. 'Seriously, Umari, you're such a scaredy-cat!'

'Guys, knock it off!' Sani snapped, glaring at them. 'If you don't quit teasing, I'm telling Dad tomorrow. And trust me, he's not gonna think it's funny.'

Sani was the second eldest brother, but his height and serious demeanour made him seem like the pack's leader.

Abner, though the eldest, seldom behaved like it. As the group's storyteller, he thrived on spinning wild tales of zombies, ghosts, and monsters. It was his brilliant idea to lead them into the Moonlit Marshes, convinced they'd uncover proof of the undead.

Ray, the third brother, was the mischief-maker. His favourite hobbies included teasing his brothers, cracking jokes, and making Umari squirm. No matter how creepy the situation, he could find a joke in anything.

Then there was Umari, the youngest. Despite being the troublemaker most of the time, he was terrified of the dark. The rustling leaves, the fog, and Abner's stories had him casting wary glances at every shifting shadow.

'Did you hear that?' Ray whispered sharply, stopping in his tracks. His eyes scanned the darkness, his complexion turning ashen.

'What?' Abner hissed, spinning around, his eyes straining to pierce through the heavy mist.

'We need to leave,' Umari muttered, his voice shaking as he clutched Sani's arm.

Sani swung the flashlight in wide arcs, the beam slicing through the swirling fog but revealing nothing.

Ray suddenly burst into laughter, the sound breaking the tense silence. 'Gotcha!' he cackled, his grin wide. 'You should've seen your faces!'

'You idiot!' Umari snapped, his fear spilling over into anger. As he shouted, flecks of spit flew from his mouth, landing squarely on Ray's face.

'Ew! Gross!' Ray yelled, wiping his face frantically. 'That's disgusting!' He hit Umari hard on the shoulder, but before Umari could swing back, a sharp *hiss* sliced through the air.

The group froze.

'What...what was that?' Umari stammered, his fist still poised defensively, his gaze flickering in every direction. Then, with a terrified shriek, he sprinted through the thick fog.

'Aaaagh!' Abner screamed, his voice trembling with fear. His eyes were fixed on the ground ahead. Through the haze of mist, a muddy, filthy hand was pushing its way up from the ground, clawing at the air like it was trying to reach them.

'Let's get out of here!' Ray yelled, turning around and sprinting in the direction Umari had gone.

'Get a grip,' Sani chuckled nervously, though the beads of sweat on his forehead betrayed his unease. 'Zombies aren't real. It's probably just a branch or something.'

But just as he spoke, the ground in front of them split open, and dozens of grey, muddy hands started to claw their way up. Battered and uneven, their fingernails were caked with dried blood, the edges bent and splintered, and the sound of cracking bones filled the air.

Sani let out a sharp scream and dropped the flashlight; it hit the ground and shattered. The bulb burst, glass shards scattering everywhere, and suddenly, everything was plunged into darkness.

Abner grabbed Sani's arm, and the two of them stumbled backwards, their feet squelching into the wet ground as they moved towards the safety of the dense bushes. Their bodies shook with fear.

One by one, heads began to rise from the earth, their green, slimy hair dripping down their pale, lifeless faces. Many were missing yellowed teeth, but most unsettling of all, their eyes remained shut tight as if they couldn't see but were still searching blindly.

The grey zombies started to swing their heads from side to side, sniffing the air as if hunting for a scent.

Sani's voice trembled. 'So, what should you do if you see *The Zombies of the Moonlit Marshes*?'

'I-I don't know!' Abner said, his voice rising in panic.

All at once, the zombies' heads turned towards Sani and Abner, their eyes snapping open with a lifeless, hollow stare. Their mouths hung open, dripping with hunger, as their decaying hands reached out, slow and unrelenting.

'RUN!' Sani shouted, panic creeping into his voice. Without hesitation, they both bolted, their legs aching as they tore through the marsh.

'What do you mean you don't know what to do if you see a zombie?' Sani snapped, his breath coming fast and shallow. 'You're the one who dragged us here to find them! What was your *plan* if we actually found them?' His words came out in gasps as the sound of heavy, sloshing footsteps closed in behind them.

'W-well, I was just messing around,' Abner gasped, his heart thudding painfully against his ribs. 'I didn't think they were real!'

Sani's jaw dropped, eyes wide in disbelief. 'WHAT?!'

The wind howled, carrying with it the sound of heavy, wet footsteps growing closer and closer. The zombies were chasing them, and their footsteps sounded like thunder, getting louder with every heartbeat.

Chapter Three

'Where are Sani and Abner?' Umari whispered, pressing his back against the rough bark of an old oak tree.

'I'm not sure,' Ray panted, his breath visible in the frigid air. 'They were just standing there, staring at the hand rising from the dirt, as if they were frozen in shock.'

'I think they've been eaten,' Umari stammered, his voice trembling and barely audible. His wide, frightened eyes revealed the depth of his fear.

'That can't be true,' Ray said, his voice shaky but laced with a desperate attempt at bravery for his little brother. Deep down, though, he couldn't shake the gut-wrenching fear that his older brothers were in grave danger.

'What do we do now?' Umari whispered, his voice trembling as tears brimmed in his eyes.

Before Ray could answer, a sudden hissing voice slithered through the air, cold and menacing: 'RUN!'

'Aaagh!' Ray and Umari's terrified cries split the night, their hurried footsteps a frantic rhythm in the dark.

They stumbled over roots and branches, crashing into rocks that scraped their knees, but they didn't dare stop. Whatever was behind them was fast - and it sounded hungry.

Umari's spine tingled as a low, menacing growl reached his ears. A sharp branch whipped across his face, scratching him, but he barely noticed, his panic urging him to keep running.

Ray was ahead, sprinting like a madman, his legs throbbing with every step. His breath came in ragged gasps, but he didn't slow down, not with the sound of snapping twigs and heavy footsteps closing in behind them.

Suddenly, Umari's jacket snagged on a branch, yanking him backwards and sending him sprawling into the mud. His elbows scraped against sharp rocks, and he cried out in pain. 'Ray! Help me!' he sobbed, tears streaming down his cheeks as he watched Ray's figure vanish into the thick fog.

'Don't leave me!' Umari cried, his voice trembling with desperation. 'Ray! Please!'

Crack!

The sudden snap of a twig shattered the air, cutting his cries short. His breath faltered, and his wide, fearful eyes swept over the shadows. Then, out of nowhere, a grey figure lunged, its force knocking him flat into the thick, wet mud.

Umari let out a bloodcurdling scream, his heart pounding as he locked eyes with the creature's glowing red gaze. Its decayed, mud-caked face loomed ever closer, its torn lips twisting into a grotesque grin.

'Don't eat me, you zombie!' he shouted, voice trembling with terror. He thrashed wildly, clawing at the mud as he fought to free himself, searching for anything he could use to fight off the attacker. His fingers finally closed around a thick branch.

'Yummy, you'll be delicious to eat,' the zombie hissed, licking its cracked, slimy lips with a tongue as grey as its skin.

Umari wasn't about to let himself become a midnight snack. With a terrified yell, he swung the branch with all his might, smacking the zombie square in the head. It stumbled back, growling low and deep, its red eyes fixed on him as if deciding how to strike again.

Umari scrambled to his feet, his legs shaking like jelly. He gripped the branch tightly, his knuckles white. The zombie shook its filthy head, its slimy green hair clinging to its bony face like dripping slugs.

'You're gonna be my yummy dinner,' the zombie rasped, its cracked lips curling into a creepy grin.

'And you're gonna be my baseball!' Umari shot back, his voice shaking. With all his strength, he swung the branch, whacking the zombie straight in the face. The horrible creature flew backwards with a loud grunt, landing in the mud.

But it didn't stay down. With a guttural growl, the zombie lunged forward like a charging bull; its filthy hands stretched out to grab him.

A shiver raced down Umari's spine. He dropped the branch and bolted, his legs pumping as fast as they could. 'HELP!' he screamed, tears streaming down his cheeks. His voice trembled as he cried, his mouth hanging open, drool dripping out as he darted through the trees like a panicked rabbit.

Umari glanced over his shoulder quickly, only to crash straight into a tree. Stars exploded in his vision, and he crumpled to the ground, dazed and groaning.

'Got ya now,' the zombie sneered, its thin, grimy hands stretching towards Umari like a deathly promise.

'Get away from my brother, you idiot!'

Umari's eyes darted behind the zombie, and he saw Ray standing there, holding something shiny in his hand.

The zombie spun around, its blood-smeared lips twisting into a cruel smile. 'What're you gonna do with that fake gun?' it growled. Then, with a hiss, it charged at Ray.

Ray screamed, his heart pounding in his chest. Without thinking, he pulled the trigger. A blast of water shot from the nozzle and splattered the zombie directly in the eye.

The creature staggered back, screaming in shock, wiping its eye furiously. Ray blinked, his mouth dry. Was the zombie afraid of water? But how could that be? They were standing in the middle of a marsh.

Ray pressed the trigger again, and a stream of water shot out, hitting the zombie in the cheek. It howled and stumbled, its greasy hair whipping around its face.

'Ha, take that!' Ray shouted, squirting more water at its filthy body. 'And this!' He aimed at the zombie's chest, soaking it with another blast.

The zombie let out a painful cry, its body crumpling to the ground and dissolving into a nasty, murky green puddle. Only its hands remained, twitching and crawling in the mud.

'Oh gosh, that was scary,' Umari whimpered, pushing himself to his feet, his knees still shaking.

'Aagh!' Ray screamed as the zombie's hands suddenly jerked to life. One of them clamped down on his leg, its long, jagged nails digging into his skin like hooks. Ray gasped in pain and tried to shake it off, but the hand held tight, pulling him towards the ground.

Chapter Four

Abner and Sani raced through the muddy marsh, their boots sinking into the mud with every frantic step. Behind them, the creepy groans of zombies thundered through the air.

'What do we do now?!' Abner shouted, his voice barely rising above the shrieking wind. His heart hammered in his chest, its rhythm deafening in his ears.

'I-I don't kn...' Sani's words were cut off as he suddenly tripped, his legs giving way as he plunged face-first into a deep puddle of muck. The marsh sucked him down like a hungry beast.

'Sani!' Abner froze in terror, his eyes wide as he watched his brother sink into the mud, his body slowly vanishing like a stone in quicksand. 'Sani! Take my hand!' Abner shouted, stumbling forward, his breath coming in sharp, desperate gasps.

'Take my hand!' Abner repeated, his voice breaking with panic as his hand shook, reaching desperately towards his brother. Sani's face was buried in the mud, his body sinking lower and lower, disappearing inch by inch into the thick, clinging muck. He tried to lift his hand, but the mud was like sticky slime, pulling him deeper and trapping him like a spider's web.

Suddenly, the earth beneath Sani gave way with a sickening crack, collapsing into a yawning hole.

Abner's heart raced as he turned around, his eyes widening in terror. The zombies had almost caught up to him - at least a hundred of them, their skin rotting and peeling away. Their bony hands reached out towards him, long, gnarled fingers stretching like claws, and blood oozed from their open, decayed mouths.

Every time they breathed, a foul green mist escaped, swirling in the air around them.

Abner stared wide-eyed at the big, dark hole in the ground. His heart thumped loudly in his chest, and he felt a little dizzy. But his brother needed him, and Abner wasn't about to give up! He clenched his fists, took a deep breath, and whispered, 'I can do this.'

With one giant leap, he jumped into the hole. The wind roared past him, tossing his hair in every direction, while the darkness closed in around him, heavy and suffocating like a thick, woollen blanket.

He opened his eyes in panic and saw a blur of jagged rocks racing past him.

'Yiiiiiikes!' The word tore from his throat as he plummeted into the unknown, the ground rushing up to meet him.

With a sudden jolt, he landed with a soft thud. He blinked, disoriented, then slowly sat up. His heart pounded in his chest, but relief washed over him as he exhaled. 'That wasn't a bad landing.'

'Cause your skinny butt landed on me.'

Abner looked down in surprise, then quickly jumped to his feet. 'Oops! Sorry, Sani!' he said, offering a hand to help him up. 'I didn't mean to land on you,' he added, trying hard not to laugh.

Sani swatted Abner's hand away and stood up, wiping slimy mud off his knees. 'This is gross,' he grumbled, scrunching his face as he tried to comb the mud out of his hair with his fingers.

'Where are we, anyway?' Abner asked as he looked around at his surroundings.

'You're the one who brought us here! You should know,' Sani shot back, his gaze scanning what seemed like a massive cave.

Abner froze. 'Did you hear that?'

'What?!' Sani asked, grabbing a small pebble from the ground.

'Aagh, let go of me!' came a muffled voice.

'Oh no!' Sani gasped, swallowing hard. 'That sounds like Ray!'

Sani and Abner tiptoed towards the noise, their footsteps barely making a sound. They turned a corner and saw a huge rocky slope leading up to the cave's ceiling. Two figures tumbled down the slope, their bodies twisting and turning as they fell.

Abner squinted. 'Is that...?' His words trailed off as the two figures slammed into the ground in a tangled heap.

'Ray! Umari!' Sani and Abner yelled in a mix of relief and disbelief.

'Get these hands off us!' Ray shrieked, desperately clawing at the bony hand gripping his leg.

Umari, who was also struggling with a hand latched onto his leg, shouted, 'It hates water! Squirt it with your water gun!'

Abner and Sani exchanged a quick, worried glance before pulling their water guns from their pants pockets. Abner aimed and shot at the hand clinging to Ray's leg, while Sani did the same for the one on Umari's leg.

'Whoa, it's working!' Abner said, squinting as the hands started to dissolve. 'They're melting away!'

The boys kept squirting water until the hands finally dropped off Ray and Umari's legs, turning into a strange green liquid that splattered on the ground.

'How did you know they don't like water?' Sani asked, helping Umari to his feet.

'Forget that!' Umari yelled, his eyes wide with fear as he stared up at the ceiling. 'RUN!'

Sani and Abner looked up just in time to see hundreds of zombies falling from the massive hole in the cave's roof.

The four of them sprinted, their hearts racing, breaths sharp and uneven.

'What are we supposed to do?!' Ray yelled, panic rising in his voice. 'How are we supposed to survive this? I wish I wasn't here! I wish I were on another continent...Africa, maybe! There's probably no zombies there!' He shouted over the sound of footsteps pounding behind them, the horde closing in.

'Get them!' a raspy voice hissed, and suddenly, the whole swarm of zombies let out a bone-chilling hiss like a thousand serpents preparing to strike.

Abner's eyes widened in horror as he looked ahead. 'Has this just gotten a *lot* worse?' he gulped, his breath coming in rapid, shallow gasps as a surge of zombies barrelled towards them from the front.

'Turn this way!' Sani shouted, his voice sharp as he veered into a narrow rocky tunnel, barely wide enough for them all to squeeze through.

Umari, trailing behind the others, yelled, 'We're gonna end up as zombie snacks!'

Ray screamed, his voice wild, 'And then we'll get pooped out in a zombie toilet!'

Chapter Five

The zombies were closing in rapidly, their screams growing louder as they charged from behind.

'In here!' Abner cried, squeezing through a jagged crack in the stone wall with desperate haste.

Sani followed, diving through the small opening with the grace of a swimmer. Not quite as graceful, Ray tried to do the same, but his knee slammed into the wall as he leapt. 'Ouch!' he yelped, his teeth sinking into his lip, the sharp pain growing more intense with each passing second.

But it was too late for Umari. A zombie's cold, clammy hands grabbed him by the shoulders, yanking him away from the hole and dragging him into the darkness.

Abner wiped the dust off his hands as he stood up. 'I think we lost them,' he whispered, glancing over at Sani, who was removing his shoe to shake out a stone.

'That was way too close,' Sani mumbled, slipping his shoe back on.

'I hit my knee *really* hard,' Ray grumbled, teeth clenched, his face contorted like an angry, roaring dinosaur. 'Stupid zombies,' he spat, emphasising the word *stupid* - a habit of his whenever he was frustrated.

'Wait,' Abner said suddenly, his voice sharp. 'Where's Umari?'

'Oh no!' Sani gasped, his face pale with worry. 'This is bad. This is *really* bad.'

'He's gonna end up as zombie food!' Ray yelled, his voice trembling while his lips quivered and his face turned ghostly pale.

'We have to find him, *now*,' Sani said, clenching his fists, determination flooding his eyes.

'But how are we going to do that?' Ray groaned, looking around helplessly.

'We've got our water guns. We can blast them away,' Abner said, trying to stay optimistic.

'Are you *seriously* mashed in the head?!' Sani yelled, his frustration bubbling over. 'There are millions of zombies, and we have only three water guns. How can we possibly hope to defend ourselves with such few weapons? The water's going to run out!'

'Excuse me,' Ray interrupted, raising a hand to pause the conversation. 'We only have *two* water guns. I dropped mine when that ugly, slimy, stinky, bony, filthy, horrifying, absolutely grimy hand grabbed my leg,' he said, shaking his head in disgust.

'That's even more brilliant,' Sani muttered, his voice dripping with sarcasm.

'You're so pathetic! Why did you drop it?!' Abner shouted, throwing his hands up in exasperation.

'You're the one who's pathetic! We wouldn't be in this mess if you hadn't dragged us here!' Ray shot back, his face red with anger.

'Hey, *you* agreed to come here! *You* convinced me!' Abner bellowed.

'No, I didn't, you idiot...' Ray started, but Sani interrupted.

'Shut up, both of you!' he growled, his voice rumbling through the narrow hole. 'If we keep arguing, we're never going to get Umari back. We need to focus!'

'Yeah, you're right,' Abner said, narrowing his eyes, his mind shifting back to the task.

'Okay, let's get our bro and take down those bald-headed creeps!' Ray said, striking a ridiculously dramatic fist in the air like he was in a movie.

'Uhh...they're not bald, Ray. They've got green hair and...'

'Please don't start the 'who's bald and who's not' debate!' Sani snapped, rolling his eyes and then quickly peeking through the hole. 'Guys,' he whispered, looking back at Ray and Abner. 'There's not even one zombie in sight. Let's get moving.'

'Yeah, they're probably all in some giant zombie kitchen, getting ready to cook *The Umari Special*... with extra brains and a side of *mashed twinkle toes*',' Abner said, doing air quotes.

Sani squeezed through the hole, with Abner and Ray following closely behind.

'This is scary,' Ray stammered, his voice trembling. 'I wish I could be back in my cosy bed at home,' he said, wrapping his arms around his waist.

'Don't worry,' Sani said, placing a reassuring hand on Ray's shoulder. 'We'll get our brother back and make it home safely. I promise,' he said, offering a shaky smile that didn't ease the tension.

Ray didn't feel comforted. A cold shiver ran down his spine. How were they going to stand a chance against a million zombies? And who knew how many more might be lurking in the shadows?

They continued through the winding cave, their eyes darting nervously in the thick darkness, every step heavier than the last.

Finally, Abner broke the tense silence, his voice low. 'I wish we still had our flashlight. But no, someone dropped it, and now it's broken,' he sighed, glancing at Sani.

'Shh!' Ray hissed urgently. 'Don't talk. Keep your ears open. We need to find those bald heads,' he said, eyes darting frantically around the darkness.

Abner grunted in frustration. 'Are you serious? They're not bald. They've got hair.'

'Forget him,' Sani cut in, trying to stay focused. 'You know he calls everything he hates a bald head,' he sighed, turning sharply around a bend. Abner rolled his eyes, and Ray shot him an irritating grin.

The cave was abruptly filled with an eerie, hollow laughter that seemed to come from everywhere and nowhere, causing them to freeze in fear.

'What is that dreadful noise?' Ray whispered, his voice trembling.

'Forget the noise. What's that disgusting smell?' Abner asked, wrinkling his nose.

Sani sniffed the air, his face twisting in disgust. 'Yuck, it...it smells like...' He stopped, unsure if he really wanted to say it.

'It smells like f-f-firrrrrrrrrrrrrrre!' Ray screamed.

Chapter Six

'*Fire!* Where is that smell coming from? I can't see any flames,' Abner said, his voice trembling with panic as his eyes darted frantically in every direction.

Ray took a deep sniff, his face twisted in thoughtful scrutiny. 'Hey, guys…' he whispered, his voice barely audible. 'I think it's coming from this direction.' He gestured towards his right, then turned and began walking towards the source of the smell. The others hurried after him, their hearts pounding with anticipation.

As they continued walking, the smell grew stronger, and the air thickened with smoke, making breathing harder. 'Oh boy,' Ray coughed.

Sani and Abner caught up to him, and their jaws dropped in shock. They were standing at the edge of a massive cliff, peering down into a deep, dark trench. The figures below were barely visible, but the movement was unmistakable.

'*Zombies!*' Ray screamed, his voice high and filled with terror, his legs unsteady as he stumbled backwards.

Sani acted fast, slapping a hand over Ray's mouth and hissing through his teeth, 'Shut up, you're gonna draw attention!'

'I think the *dope* has already drawn attention,' Abner muttered, his voice filled with panic.

Two zombies, their eyes dull and hands tightly gripping spears, began to shuffle towards them with slow, calculated movements. 'Get them!' one of them snarled, its voice strained. They surged forward in a sudden, relentless charge.

The zombie with matted red hair lunged at Ray, slamming him to the ground with terrifying force. Ray struggled beneath the weight, but the zombie's grip was too firm. It raised a spear above its head, the jagged point aimed straight for Ray's chest.

'This is the end of you, little boy,' it growled in a guttural voice. Just as the spear was about to plunge down, the zombie hissed in pain, its body jerking back. 'What was that?' it growled, its green eyes darting towards the left. They locked onto Abner, who stood with a water gun in his hand, his fingers trembling but determined.

'Back off, you ugly scum!' Abner shouted, his voice steady despite the fear gnawing at him. He quickly pressed the trigger again.

A powerful stream of water blasted into the zombie's face. It screamed, a horrible gurgling sound, as the water hit its rotten skin. The zombie's nose began to bubble and melt, its flesh turning into a disgusting green slime. The goo dripped down its face, pooling on the ground with a sickening squelch. The smell immediately hit them - like rotting meat mixed with something foul and burnt.

The zombie let out a horrible screech as its face disintegrated. The slime continued to melt, sliding down its body in thick, gooey streaks. Within moments, it was reduced to a puddle of putrid green liquid, the stink so overwhelming it made Ray gag.

'That's one zombie down,' Abner said, panting, his voice shaky but triumphant. 'But we need to move. Now.'

Sani faced the other zombie, his heart pounding in his chest. Without hesitation, he squeezed the trigger of his water gun. A gush of water shot out, splattering across the zombie's arm. The moment the water made contact, its rotting flesh began to dissolve, the skin bubbling and turning to goo. The zombie let out a gurgling cry, its grip on the spear loosening as its fingers crumbled away. The weapon slipped from its dissolving hand, clattering to the ground.

Abner wasted no time. He aimed his water gun straight at the zombie's face and squeezed the trigger. A powerful stream of water hit the zombie with full force, and in an instant, its head began to collapse, the once horrifying features melting away into a disgusting slosh of green goo. The zombie crumpled to the floor with a sickening splat, its body rapidly dissolving into a stinking, slimy puddle of liquid.

'That was *terrifying!*' Ray gasped, wiping the sweat off his brow with a shaky hand.

'*Help me!*' came a desperate cry.

They whirled around, hearts pounding with terror. To their astonishment, a thick rope hung from the ceiling of the immense cave, hooked onto a jagged rock. At the rope's end, bound tightly, was Umari.

'Oh no,' Abner muttered, his eyes widening in horror as he peered over the cliff's edge. Below, he saw zombies dancing around a crackling fire, their twisted movements jerky and grotesque. A very ugly-looking zombie slowly released the rope, lowering Umari dangerously close to the scorching flames.

'We've got to act fast!' Sani yelled, his voice urgent. Without thinking, he shot off like a bullet train, racing towards the cliff's edge.

'Don't tell me that crazy nut is going to jump off and grab the rope!' Ray gasped, his mouth hanging open in disbelief as he watched Sani sprint forward.

Ray and Abner squeezed their eyes shut, bracing for the worst. The seconds stretched into what felt like an eternity. When they didn't hear a scream or the sickening thud of Sani hitting the ground, they cautiously opened their eyes.

Sani was hanging onto the rope, his knuckles white with the effort, his body swaying slightly in the air. He looked down at Umari, his voice steady but filled with determination. 'Hold on, lil' bro, I'm right here,' he called out, his voice steady despite the danger.

Umari's eyes were wide with terror as he looked up at Sani, his face drenched in sweat. 'H-help me!' he squeaked, his voice trembling like a frightened mouse.

Chapter Seven

Sani gazed up at the rope tied to the jagged rock, his heart pounding urgently. He gritted his teeth and yanked on it with all his strength. The rope creaked as he swung forward. He pushed harder, his feet kicking the air, and suddenly, he was soaring side to side like he was on the world's most dangerous swing.

The rope creaked and groaned as he swung back and forth, the movement so wild it was almost ridiculous. He was flinging himself back and forth to the left, then the right, barely keeping his grip on the rope. The zombies below were watching with a mix of confusion and disappointment. Their heads moved slowly from one side to the other, tracking Sani's clumsy, erratic swings as if they were watching a terrible show.

'Seriously?' one zombie groaned, shaking its head, clearly unimpressed.

But Sani wasn't slowing down. He swung harder, his body flying through the air, higher and higher with each swing, the wind whooshing past his ears.

Ray and Abner watched with wide eyes. 'W-what in the world of zombies is he trying to do?' Ray asked, his voice trembling.

Then, with one massive swing to the left, Sani let out a yell and went flying even higher. The rope creaked dangerously, and with a *snap*, it suddenly came loose from the jagged rock. Sani flew through the air like a wild superhero, his arms and legs going in all directions, before he finally crashed with a *thud* onto the cliffside in a tangled heap of limbs and rope.

'OMG!' Abner yelled. 'Are you all right?' He sprinted over to Sani, his eyes wide with panic.

'Forget about me! We need to pull the rope to get Umari up!' Sani urgently said, scrambling to his feet, his hands gripping the rope tightly.

Ray and Abner nodded, grabbing the rope. 'Alright, on the count of three, we pull,' Sani shouted, his voice filled with determination.

'ONE... TWO... THREE... PULL!'

They yanked with all their strength. The rope creaked under the pressure, but they didn't stop. They pulled harder, their muscles burning with the effort.

Umari's body slowly began to rise, inch by inch, his wide, terrified eyes locked onto his brothers. The zombies below began to take notice, their hisses growing louder, but the kids didn't stop.

'Keep going! Just a little more!' Sani shouted, his voice strained from the effort. Sweat dripped from his brow as he pulled with everything he had.

With one final, powerful tug, Umari was hauled safely onto the cliff's edge.

'YES!' Ray and Abner shouted, a wave of relief crashing over them.

Sani dropped to his knees, gasping for air. 'We did it...we really did it...'

Umari looked up, tears in his eyes. 'You guys...you saved me.' His voice trembled with gratitude, and he hugged Sani tightly.

'WE NEED TO GET OUT OF HERE! NOW!' Abner shouted, his eyes wide as he looked down the cliff. The zombies were scrambling up the rocks, their hands clawing at the stone with unnerving speed, their growls growing louder with each passing second.

'Oh, this is NOT good!' Ray yelled, his voice filled with panic. 'Let's RUN!'

The four boys bolted, their feet thudding loudly against the rocky ground as they raced through the dark cave. Their hearts pounded furiously, but the sound of the zombies' growls only pushed them harder.

'We can't just keep running,' Sani shouted, his voice trembling. 'If we do, we'll get tired, and they'll catch up to us and…'

'A-a-a-and turn us into zombie food!' Umari stammered, his breath coming out in sharp gasps, his legs barely keeping up with Ray's.

'We need a plan!' Abner panted, sweat beading on his forehead. He stole a quick glance over his shoulder. The zombies were getting closer, their glowing eyes shining in the dark.

'We know that zombies melt with water, but we don't have any left!' Ray gasped, his chest heaving with every breath. Sweat poured down his face, stinging his eyes.

'We need to run towards the deserted farmyard!' Sani shouted.

'Why?!' Abner yelled, his voice nearly drowned out by the deafening sound of the zombies' thunderous footsteps pounding behind them.

'I saw water hoses!' Sani shouted, his eyes wide with determination. 'We can blast them with water - clear them off planet Earth!'

'But what if the hoses don't work?!' Ray shouted back, his voice shaky as the noise of hundreds of zombies echoed all around them, their growls and shrieks reverberating off the cave walls.

'It's worth a try!' Abner said, glancing over his shoulder. The sight of the horde chasing them was enough to freeze anyone with fear. Their eyes glowed like fireflies in the dark, their twisted bodies moving with unnatural speed. They were getting closer with every second, their rotting hands reaching out, scraping the stone walls as they ran.

Chapter Eight

The four brothers pushed harder with every stride, running as fast as the wind. The sound of zombies' feet pounding behind them was relentless and terrifying. The cave around them twisted and turned like a maze, the walls closing in. Panting heavily, they couldn't afford to slow down - the zombies were gaining ground.

A steep rocky slope appeared ahead of them, and without hesitation, they scrambled towards it. Their hands scraped against the jagged rocks, and their feet slipped on loose gravel as they made their way up.

'Faster!' Sani shouted, his voice hoarse as he gripped a sharp rock and pulled himself up.

Suddenly, with a gut-wrenching jolt, Ray felt something clamp around his leg - a zombie had seized him!

'Get off me, you idiot!' Ray shouted, struggling to free his leg as the zombie's bony fingers dug into his flesh.

He delivered a powerful kick, his boot striking the zombie's face with precision. The creature let out a guttural shriek, toppling backwards and sliding down the rocky slope before crashing to the ground with a harsh, sickening thud.

'Not today, pal,' Ray muttered, scrambling up the rocks. As his brothers ascended the slope, they called out, urging him to follow.

They finally reached the top and, without hesitation, slipped through a narrow gap in the rocky wall - just wide enough to squeeze through. The biting cold night air struck them like a harsh slap, but they pressed on, ignoring the chill and the fierce wind howling around them, clawing at their skin. They couldn't stop now; they had to keep running.

The moon hung low in the sky, casting an eerie glow over the land. The wind howled, whipping through the trees as they dashed across the vast, muddy marsh. Their shoes sank into the muck with every step, but they didn't care. Mud splashed on their clothes and legs, but they had no time to worry about the mess, not with the zombies closing in.

'Why are the zombies scared of water?' Umari stammered, trying to keep up with his brothers. 'This grimy marsh water basically surrounds them!'

'I dunno, dude!' Abner shouted back, his voice filled with frustration and panic. 'Maybe they're allergic to the water we use or something, but we're gonna have to figure that out later!'

The cold, sticky mud clung to their shoes, dragging them down with every step, but they pushed forward, not caring. Their only goal was to reach the farmyard ahead.

They reached the swamp's edge and dashed straight across, not caring if their pants got soaked. The swamp stretched forever, the cold water splashing around their ankles as they raced through the muck. After what felt like ages, they finally emerged from the swamp, bursting into the deserted farmyard. In the distance, the silhouette of the old, creaky barn loomed against the glowing moonlight, its shadow stretching across the ground.

'That's it!' Ray yelled, pointing towards the barn. 'We've got to make it to that barn!'

They didn't waste a second. With their hearts pounding, they bolted across the farmyard. The barn loomed closer and closer, its broken-down structure creaking in the wind like it might fall apart at any moment. But it was their only shot at survival.

'We're almost there!' Sani yelled, his voice full of determination as they sprinted towards the barn's creaky door.

The four of them skidded to a halt in front of the barn's battered door, their hearts hammering. To the left of the barn, five old hose pipes hung limply from rusty metal taps bolted to a weather-beaten wall. The ground beneath them suddenly trembled, faint at first but quickly growing into a violent shudder.

'What now?' Ray gasped, turning his face towards the swamp.

Chapter Nine

The answer came in a gut-wrenching roar. Emerging from the murky shadows, a tide of zombies thundered through the swamp, their grotesque forms moving faster than before. Ragged, torn flesh hung off their bodies, their empty, glowing eyes locked onto the children. They shrieked and howled, a horrifying sound that pierced the night and sent chills racing down their spines.

'They're right behind us!' Umari screamed, grabbing Sani's arm.

The horrible horde tore across the swamp, their feet slapping against the muddy water. They were less than twenty meters away, closing in fast.

'Those pipes!' Sani shouted, pointing to the taps. 'It's our only shot!'

They dashed towards the taps, their muddy shoes slipping on the trembling ground. Sani kept a watchful eye on the approaching zombies while the other three brothers yanked on the rusted taps with all their strength, but they wouldn't budge.

'Move!' Sani yelled, shoving past Abner to take the lead. His hands clamped down on the first tap, and with a mighty yank, he forced it open. Water gushed from the hose in a sputtering hiss, shooting out in chaotic, unpredictable bursts.

Sani grabbed the next tap, his muscles straining against the rust. The zombies were only ten meters away now, their growls vibrating in the air. Another tap broke free, water gushing through the hose in a sudden torrent.

'Grab it!' Sani instructed, tossing it to Abner before moving to the next.

He wrenched the remaining taps open one by one. Umari and Ray grabbed their hoses, their hands trembling as they stared at the monstrous wave of undead charging towards them.

'They're only two meters away!' Abner shouted, his voice breaking with terror.

'Spray them!' Sani roared, clutching his hose and aiming it at the zombies.

The powerful streams hit the leading zombies, drenching their faces and chests. The creatures unleashed blood-curdling screams, their rotting skin bubbling and peeling like hot wax under a flame. As the torrents of water lashed against them, chunks of decayed flesh sloughed off, revealing green, oozing muscle underneath.

A zombie's arm dropped to the ground with a sickening *splat*, twitching briefly before disintegrating into a puddle of slimy green goo. Another creature's nose melted away, leaving a cavernous hole that dripped with sickly fluid. A towering zombie let out a rumbling roar as its head began to dissolve, caving in like a collapsing sandcastle before streaming down its body in grotesque rivulets.

'Eww!' Umari shrieked, his stomach turning. 'It's like the world's grossest smoothie!'

The kids didn't have time to process the horror as hundreds more zombies surged forward from the swamp, their howls echoing through the night. The ground shook as the mass of creatures charged at them, but the kids held their ground, the water jets blasting through the dark like laser beams.

One by one, the zombies were struck and dissolved into oozing heaps of green sludge. Some screamed and twitched as their torsos dissolved, leaving only skeletal remains that collapsed into the muck. Others charged forward with missing limbs or no heads, only to be obliterated by another blast of water.

'This is so nasty!' Ray shouted, twisting his hose wildly. 'It's like a giant snot-factory explosion!'

'You're not helping, Ray!' Abner yelled back, moving quickly as a zombie's slimy hand flew off and landed with a *splat* near his feet.

'Do you think this water's made of zombie soap or something?' Umari asked, laughing despite the chaos.

'Zombie soap?!' Sani snorted as he adjusted his aim. 'What's next? Zombie shampoo?'

Ray grinned. 'I mean, they *could* use a bath! Look at them, this is probably the first time they've seen clean water!'

'Less jokes, more melting!' Sani shouted, but even he struggled to keep a straight face as another zombie's head popped like a water balloon.

'Hey, look!' Abner yelled, aiming his hose at a particularly fat zombie. It exploded into green goo mid-stride, splattering the others behind it. 'We're making zombie smoothies! Who's up for round two?'

'No way,' Umari said, wrinkling his nose. 'But I think Ray doesn't mind!'

Ray squirted a jet of water into the air, drenching another wave of zombies. 'I'll have my smoothie with extra sludge, please!'

As the horde grew smaller, their horrifying screams were replaced by the squelching sounds of melting flesh and bubbling goo. The kids, still spraying water, couldn't help but laugh and crack jokes, even as their arms started to tire.

'This is the weirdest water fight ever!' Abner laughed, exchanging a mischievous grin with his brothers.

'I thought science experiments were gross,' Umari muttered, aiming his hose at a zombie clawing its way forward despite having no legs.

'This is disgusting but fantastic,' Ray said with a dramatic gasp, 'I think we just invented zombie art! Check out that goo sculpture!'

The brothers couldn't hold back their laughter, their commentary cutting through the tension. A final blast cleared the last zombie, leaving the farmyard unnervingly quiet.

They stood panting, surrounded by puddles of green sludge, their clothes splattered with mud and muck.

Sani wiped the sweat from his brow, smiling. 'Well, I guess that's one way to clear out a zombie infestation.'

Ray raised his hose like a trophy, grinning from ear to ear. 'Why do adults always say water fights are a baby game and they'll never come in handy for the future?!' He gestured dramatically at the piles of green sludge around them. 'Mum, if you were here to see this, you'd be proud...I think!'

Abner rolled his eyes. 'Yeah, I'm sure she'll be really proud when she sees your report card covered in zombie guts.'

'Hey, priorities!' Ray shot back. 'Saving the world always comes first, then homework.'

Chapter Ten

Umari woke with a yawn, stretching his arms and rubbing his eyes. He pushed off the blankets and sat up, his groggy gaze shifting to his brothers, who were starting to stir in their beds.

'Guys, that was a *crazy* night,' Umari muttered.

Ray dramatically leapt out of bed, his arms spread wide as if starring in a play. 'What night? Did I miss something epic?'

Umari sighed, rolling his eyes. 'How could you forget last night when we melted a whole horde of zombies with water?'

Sani chuckled as he sat up, his hair sticking out in all directions. 'Zombie night? What are you talking about? Wait...' He froze, his eyes suddenly widening. 'Hey, did you have the same dream as me? About...melting zombies into slime?'

'Yeah, and I had a dream about zombies chasing us through a marsh,' Ray said.

'That wasn't a dream!' Abner replied with a triumphant grin. 'It was absolutely real. We saved the world from those disgusting, stinky zombies!'

With a puzzled frown, Ray stared at his pyjamas, inspecting himself. 'Okay, but then why are we so clean? We stomped through a swamp and that gross marsh water - shouldn't we smell like old fish or something?' He sniffed his shirt, checking if it still reeked of marsh water. 'This is freaky. I'm squeaky clean?'

The room fell silent for a moment as the boys exchanged confused glances.

Sani broke the silence with a laugh, flopping back onto his pillow. 'Alright, maybe we *all* just had the same dream. Which, honestly, is weird!'

'Hey, why didn't the zombies like the water?' Umari asked, raising an eyebrow as he sat cross-legged on his bed. 'I mean, they were practically living in a wet marsh!'

Sani stood up, stretching his arms with a confident smile. 'Because monsters and scary creatures like zombies hate cleanliness. They thrive on dirt and grime, so they can't handle clean water!'

Abner nodded, his expression serious. 'So, yeah, staying clean is a must because who wants to turn into a gross zombie?'

'But was it really true what happened?' Umari asked, tilting his head. 'Did we actually save the world from zombies?'

A grin tugged at Sani's lips as he shrugged. 'I think so.'

'We're the Fearsome Four!' Ray declared, puffing out his chest like a superhero.

'Yeah,' Umari said, his face lighting up. 'We're the *Fearsome Four!*' He jumped off his bed, landing with an exaggerated pose.

'Fearsome Four!' they all yelled together, bursting into laughter as they gathered in the middle of the room for an epic group high-five. The sound of their high-five was instantly lost beneath their unrestrained laughter.

Suddenly, a sharp, deliberate *knock-knock-knock* cut through the brothers' laughter like a sharp blade.

The boys froze in place, their laughter silenced in an instant.

'W-what was that?' Umari whispered, his voice barely audible.

The knocking came again but louder this time, followed by a faint, dragging sound that sent chills down their spines. Slowly, all four of them turned their heads towards the bedroom window.

The soft morning sunlight streaming through the glass revealed something outside - a shadowy figure pressed against the windowpane. Its twisted outline was blurred, but its hollow, glowing eyes burned unnaturally.

'What on earth is that?' Ray shouted, his voice trembling with panic as he stumbled backwards.

'Is...is th-that a g-g-g...!' Umari's words caught in his throat, his trembling finger pointing at the figure. 'G-GHOOOOOOST!' he finally shrieked.

The shadow moved closer, its face pressing against the glass with a sickening *squeak*. A set of jagged, mismatched teeth flashed in a grotesque grin.

Sani stepped forward, his fists clenched with surprising determination, though his legs trembled beneath him. He squared his shoulders, trying to shake off the fear creeping up his spine. 'I-I think the *Fearsome Four* are gonna be in for a...' The knocking turned into a pounding, louder and more frantic. Sani took a deep breath, attempting to calm himself. 'A ghost hunt!' he declared, his voice firmer than before.

Upcoming Titles By Joseph Jethro:

- Fearsome Four: The Ghost of the Rickety House
- Fearsome Four: The Toad of the Grimy Underworld
- Fearsome Four: The Witch of Nightwood School
- Fearsome Four: Stenchfang the King of Poo
- Fearsome Four: The Beast of the Rocky Mountains
- Fearsome Four: The Butcher Next Door
- Fearsome Four: The Appliances of the Kitchen Downstairs
- Fearsome Four: The Captain of the Snot Monsters
- Fearsome Four: Terror Baby of the Giants